W9-COS-203

Iliana

A Winter Solstice Tale

A Children's Day Story
By Walter Fordham
Illustrated by Tatjana Krizmanic

Copyright © by Wide River Books 1995
P.O. Box 142, Central, Halifax, Nova Scotia B3J 2M4
ISBN: 0-9680007-0-3

© 1995 Walter Fordham (text and music)
© 1995 Tatjana Krizmanic (art)
Design by Stephanie Johnston
Music transcribed by Molly De Shong

All rights reserved. No part of this book may
be reproduced in any form or by any means, electronic or
mechanical, without written permission from the publisher.

For Catherine, Alicia, Peter, and William with all my love – WF

For Emilia and Katja, my two little suns – TKV

I would like to thank the children and adults who helped shape this story by reading it and listening to it as it developed and grew; Emily Sell for her skillful edits; Elizabeth Pybus for asking me to tell the story of Children's Day a long time ago; and Joanne for helping in many ways.

Most of all I would like to express my deep gratitude for Chögyam Trungpa, Rinpoche without whom many things would be different in the world. If his work and influence could be traced and catalogued it would fill many volumes. Somewhere near the back it would say that without him, this story could not be told.

– WF

THE QUEST

nce there was a girl named Iliana who lived in a high mountain valley in the Kingdom of Shambhala. She was brave and cheerful and interested in everything that she saw or heard. People said that she had big ears—not because her ears were any bigger than they should be, but because she listened to everything that people said. People said that she had big eyes— not because they were so very big, but because she noticed everything that happened.

Lately Iliana noticed that people looked unhappy. They almost never smiled and they walked with their heads low. And it seemed that wherever she went she overheard people talking in worried tones about how the sun was setting a little bit earlier every day.

One snowy night in late December when she should have been asleep, Iliana heard her parents' voices downstairs. Silently she slipped out of bed and tiptoed down the cold hall to the stairs and then, very carefully, eased herself down one step and then the next until she was sitting on the landing halfway to the living room. There she could see her parents talking by the fire. Her father was saying, "What are we going to do? Nothing like this has ever happened before. If the days keep getting shorter and shorter, there won't be any daylight left at all!"

"Surely the king and queen must see this too," said her mother. "Surely they will look after us and protect us as they always have."

Iliana could see her father's face in the firelight. It was full of sadness as he spoke. "Sweetheart, there is something that I haven't told you. Some weeks ago, the king called a meeting of his most trusted warriors and scholars. Because of my duties at the court, I was there as well. When all were gathered, His Majesty spoke of the encroaching darkness that is troubling us. He seemed as confused by the strange changes in the sun's patterns as the rest of us. At the end of the meeting the king and queen sent the strongest warriors in the kingdom on a quest to bring the sun back. But after many weeks the warriors returned looking confused and mumbling to themselves about wild animals roaming the night."

At that moment, a flash of light brightened the hallway above Iliana. But when she looked up at the hall window, all she saw was the black night through the curtains. "I must be imagining things," she thought.

Now her mother said, "But what about the court scholars? They must have some explanation for what is happening to the sun." And her father answered, "After the same meeting, the scholars met at once in the court study to talk. They talked all night and they talked all day. They are still talking. You can hear their voices echoing through the halls of the court. But they haven't found a solution."

Then once again Iliana saw a flash of light. Quietly she climbed the stairs, tiptoed down the hall and looked out the window. There was nothing but the bare winter tree limbs shaking in the wind and the moonless sky sparkling with stars. Downstairs her mother said, "We can't just wait for the sun to leave us. Someone should do something!"

Iliana sat looking at the stars. Then she saw it—a flash of lightning in the distance. "Someone must do something," she thought. The lightning flashed again and she felt as if it were calling to her. "I will go. I will do it," she said to herself. "The old stories say that the eastern path leads to the Land of the Sun. I will follow the eastern path and I will find a way to bring the sun back.

Having made her decision, Iliana was determined to go. She dressed in the warmest clothes she could find, opened the hall window and stepped carefully onto the cold slate roof. Slowly, she eased herself down the roof toward the oak tree next to the house. One strong limb reached out over the roof. She lifted herself onto it, climbed down to the lower branches and then dropped to the frozen ground—landing on her feet.

Invigorated by the cold night air, she set out at once. She had walked along the eastern path before. It ran by her house in the Kalapa Valley, climbed the steep surrounding mountains and then continued eastward across the high mountain plains. As she walked along now she thought about the old legends of the Land of the Sun. The adults thought they were just children's stories. But she knew in her heart that there really was such a place.

"The Land of the Sun is where east and west meet," Iliana repeated to herself. "A dragon as big as the sky lives there. At sunset he opens his enormous red mouth against the western horizon and swallows the sun as it leaves the daytime sky. He holds it in his belly all night and that's why the night is dark. In the morning he opens his fiery red mouth in the eastern sky and the sun rises and fills the world with light." Iliana knew that this was true because she had seen the fiery red of the dragon's mouth fill the sky every morning and evening. It was obvious to her that the dragon was responsible for the recent changes in the sun. She wondered why the warriors and scholars had not thought of that.

Although the night was cold and the snow covered her ankles, Iliana strode forward quickly. She was going on a great quest. She was going to rescue the sun and save the people of Shambhala. "How proud my parents will be when I return. I will be known as a great warrior—the girl who brought back the sun."

fter Iliana had made the climb out of the Kalapa Valley and was well along the high mountain plains, she began to notice that the path was leading her into a deep valley and the snow was getting thinner. Soon the snow was gone altogether and she walked downhill along a muddy trail until at last she came to the valley floor.

She was standing at the edge of a dark jungle. The smells of summer were in the air and she felt hot and awkward in her winter clothes. There was something about this place that she did not like. It had interrupted her journey. "I must get through this valley as quickly as possible," Iliana said aloud. She began to walk briskly with her head high—almost running along the path into the dark jungle ahead. But the root of an oak tree caught her foot and sent her flying to the ground. As the pale light of dawn spread through the jungle she found herself sitting in a small clearing. The dark shapes of the surrounding trees leaned down toward her. She felt very small. Everything was so still. Where was she? Where was the path? Alone and scared, Iliana began to cry.

But then a flash of light through the trees interrupted her tears. Iliana watched. It happened again—a burst of lightning without thunder. But in the distance—what was that sound? Someone was singing a soft and steady song. She could not hear the words at first, but after a time she heard a voice singing:

I am the tiger—
I walk on the ground.
I roam through the jungle,
I move without a sound.

The song was steady like the beating of a drum. "Could there really be a tiger?" Afraid to cry and afraid to run, Iliana watched as a huge orange tiger with black stripes stepped into the half-light of the clearing. He walked toward her, moving as gracefully as a leaf carried along on a breeze, each paw touching the earth gently as he sang:

I am the tiger—
I glide through the trees,
I move through the jungle
As soft as a breeze.

Would the tiger eat her? It was too late to run. As Iliana listened to the tiger's song and watched his gentle movements, she began to relax. She wished that she could walk like that.

I roam on the earth
And all through the night,
With smiles along my back,
I fill the sky with light.

Now one of the tiger's stripes began to glow. With a sudden burst of sparks, it leapt from his back and flashed like lightning into the sky. The tiger sang:

I am the tiger—
I walk on the ground.
I am the tiger—
With smiles all around.

Iliana wasn't afraid anymore. It seemed that the tiger wanted to help her. She got up and started to walk along behind him. She tried to make her movements like the tiger's movements, but the more she tried, the more clumsy and awkward she felt. How did he walk so steadily and gracefully? Just then the tiger sang:

If you try too hard to hurry,
You will always lag behind.
But if you want to walk like me,
You must always take your time.

Iliana tried it. She raised one leg and slowly took a step. Then she lifted the other leg and stepped forward. She moved one leg and then the next until she was walking very slowly behind the tiger. "Step, step, step," she said under her breath. She was moving along faster now—"Step, step, step." Soon she was gliding along the ground, just like the tiger.

The more carefully she stepped, the faster she moved. But when she started to enjoy the going-fast part of her walk and forgot about the stepping part, she would stumble and fall. Then she would have to start all over again—stepping slowly, gently —until she was gliding along once again behind the tiger.

In the growing light of day Iliana saw that she was once again walking along the path. Now and then one of the tiger's stripes—first one near his tail, then one along his back—would leap into the air with a flash of light. When she had walked for a long time without stumbling or tripping, the tiger stopped and sang:

Continue on your quest, young girl—
Though your challenges are great.
But don't forget this jungle path
Or the tiger's gentle gait.

What you've learned so far will guide you
As you journey far from home.
So take this gift—remember me—
As you venture on alone.

As the tiger sang, one of his stripes sparkled and glowed and leapt from his back to circle Iliana's feet. Down she looked, and what did she see? New boots—boots like the armored boots of the king's soldiers! These boots were strong and soft all at once—so strong that nothing could harm them, so soft that she could easily feel the earth beneath her feet.

When Iliana looked up, the tiger was gone. She turned and continued on her way, walking with a tiger's walk through the jungle. A steep hill loomed ahead. As she climbed up and up, the jungle grew thinner, the air became cooler, and after a time she was walking in the snow again. At the top of the hill she found fields of snow as vast as the ocean under a brilliant blue and cloudless sky. Looking back toward the tiger's jungle, all she could see was a dense fog. And if she had not known that the valley was there, she would not have guessed it now. She turned and set out eastward over the snow.

**here** were no
landmarks in the snow, no trees to mark the path, nothing to show Iliana where to go.
The morning sun was her only guide. As she walked steadily eastward, the snow grew
deeper and deeper. First it was over the tops of her new boots, then it was up to her
knees. At first her spirits were as high as the snow was deep. But she missed the tiger and
the smells of the jungle. This land of snow was barren and empty. "Will I walk on this
snow field forever?" she thought. "I walk and walk toward the east but I am no closer to
the sun than when I began. And even if I reach the Land of the Sun, how can I make the
days grow longer? Maybe I should find my way back home." On she trudged through
the snow, her doubt growing heavier and heavier.

At last she stopped walking and sat down, gazing across the ocean of snow before
her. She was about to give up and turn back when a swirling cluster of turquoise clouds
rose just over the next hill. At first there were only a few clouds. Then more and more
began to rise. As she watched them drifting in the breeze, her weariness dropped away
and with an ease that surprised her she ran up the hill with great bounding leaps through
the heavy snow. Almost before she knew it, she had reached the top of the hill. There,
down the other side, was a beautiful white lion cavorting in the snow. He frolicked and
danced and leapt about; his long white mane floated and fluttered in the wind. Like
steam, delicate plumes of mist rose from the ends of his mane. So this was the source of
the turquoise clouds! Amazed, Iliana ran to join the lion. She stumbled and rolled down
the hill and when she reached the bottom, she was covered with snow from head to foot.

Brushing away her mantle of snow, Iliana found herself face-to-face with the lion. His white fur swirled like a soft cloud along his back and sides, curling gracefully around his haunches and legs. His mane flowed elegantly in the cool breeze, as if it were made from hundreds of finely woven silk scarves. His youthful eyes sparkled playfully. This lion was the most graceful being Iliana could imagine.

The lion stood gazing down at her. Her boots caught his eye and he smiled knowingly. Then in a cheerful voice he sang:

> *I am the lion, white as snow;*
> *This cheerful world is all I know.*
> *Welcome to my mountain lair*
> *Where I roam the highlands free from care.*
>
> *All day long I've watched you walking*
> *Steady as a tiger stalking.*
> *But your face is sad, your brow is stern—*
> *There is something else that you must learn.*

With that, he began to prance gracefully through the snow, his head held high and his long mane flowing. Now he sang:

> *Your pace is good, your legs are strong,*
> *But something in your back is wrong.*
> *Your shoulders droop, your head is low.*
> *You don't enjoy the mountain snow.*
>
> *The snow is fresh, the sky is clear,*
> *There's nothing in the world to fear.*
> *So listen well to what I've said—*
> *Relax your shoulders. Lift your head!*

The lion's song made Iliana smile. As she listened, she stood straight and tall. Her lungs drank in the clean mountain air. Feeling lionlike herself, she began to prance through the snow. She felt the lion's warm breath and heard his laughter. Now he knelt behind her and with a deft nudge of his nose hoisted her onto his back. Off they flew, Iliana clinging tightly to his fur as they leapt and bounded through the snow. The lion's mane fluttered in her face and tickled her nose. Her hair danced in the cold wind and she felt as fresh and alive as the white winter day around her. "This is more like it," she thought. But what was that she felt on her head? She didn't dare let go of the lion's fur, even for a moment, to find out.

Swirling wisps of turquoise clouds arose from the lion's mane and formed graceful designs in the sky. He continued to run and sing:

I am the perky lion,
I play the whole day long.
In all my life I never give up—
I sing a cheerful song.

Finally the ride ended. The lion knelt and Iliana slid off his back. At last, reaching up to the top of her head to see what was there, she felt something hard and smooth. Off it came, and there in her hands was a warrior's helmet! It was made of gleaming white lacquered wood and there were seven snow lions delicately carved all around its sides. At the top a white silk pennant fluttered in the breeze like the lion's mane. "Is this for me?" asked Iliana. "I don't deserve so fine a gift." She tried to give it back to the lion.

The lion turned his head and looked to the west. The sun was already low on the horizon. He didn't have to say anything. Iliana knew that her task was not yet finished. Setting the helmet firmly on her head, she waved to the lion, and turned to the east. Once more, she was on her way to the Land of the Sun.

Iliana still walked with the steady pace of the tiger, but now the fluttering pennant on her helmet seemed to fly among the clouds reaching all the way to heaven. She felt tall. The earth seemed to move beneath her feet and the sky seemed to follow her as she walked along singing:

Wherever I walk the sky moves with me—
Great clouds like ships sailing at sea.
Wherever I step the ground moves with me.
We travel together: sky, earth, and me.

How tall is my helmet?
How high is the sky?
How far will I walk
On this path by and by?

THE GARUDA

With no warning,
the field of snow came to an end and Iliana stood at the edge of a high cliff. Before her, in the gathering darkness, lay vast open space. When she looked down over the edge she saw nothing but mist and clouds all the way to the eastern horizon.

There she stood in her boots and her helmet. Every bone in her body wanted to walk, to continue her journey, but there was nowhere to go. She did not know what to do. She could not bear the thought of going back and she could not go forward. Then suddenly she realized, "This must be it! This must be the Land of the Sun! This is where I will meet the dragon. Soon he will appear and I will ask him why the days are growing so short. But what will I say? I need to practice talking to him. She stood at the edge of the great cliff and said:

"Most heavenly dragon of the sky, I have come from afar to find you."

"No, that's too formal. After all, I have met the tiger and the lion already. I don't need to be shy."

"Most wonderful dragon, since I was a small child I have seen you in the sky at dawn. Now I have come to ask a favor of you."

"No no, he might think I'm being too familiar. Oh well, maybe I should just sit here and wait. Maybe he'll speak first."

Iliana sat still for a long time. Her knees ached and her back grew stiff. But there was no sign of the dragon and now it was almost dark. She leaned against a rock that was round and smooth like a giant egg. Weariness overtook her and she soon fell asleep.

When she woke up many hours later, she felt refreshed. The sky was dark and filled with stars. Iliana climbed to the top of the rock she had been leaning against and sat down with her legs crossed, her back straight and gazed eastward into the darkness.

The night went on and on. The stars moved across the sky, but there was no sign of the sun. "Maybe I'm too late," thought Iliana. "Maybe the sun is gone forever. Maybe it will never rise again! But why haven't I found the dragon? Maybe this isn't the Land of the Sun. Maybe I went the wrong way. Maybe I should . . ." Iliana sat there thinking these thoughts in the dark not knowing what to do or where to go until eventually a pale light began to spread across the eastern sky and she knew that the sun would rise after all. "So I'm not too late. Now the dragon will appear. I can almost see it!"

Iliana watched in awe as the turquoise outline of a dragon appeared near the horizon, its flaming red mouth open against the edge of the sky. But as the sun rose from the dragon's mouth and its bright light filled the world, the dragon faded—its fiery red dissolving into a bank of rose-colored clouds on the horizon.

"Wait! Dragon! Dragon! Wait! I have to talk to you," she screamed. "Come back! Please!"

Crack! The rock she had been sitting on split in two and Iliana was thrown to the ground, almost to the edge of the cliff. Out of the rock emerged a huge, fierce-looking bird with the head and wings of an eagle, the horns of a bull and the arms and torso of a man. It was twice as tall as Iliana. It spread its immense wings as if it were about to fly away and then, at the last moment, it turned and stared at Iliana with its three red eyes and laughing with a wild laugh it sang:

Do you think the sky can hear you shouting?
Do you want the sun to stop and talk?
Do you hope your hat will lift you skyward?
Do you look for a path where your boots can walk?

The path calls but you cannot follow.
The land ends and you can't go on.
Day breaks but the sun's not talking.
A dragon appears and then it's gone.

You can wait all day for the sky to answer
You can walk all your life from land to land.
Though your boots are strong and your hat is splendid.
You will never meet the dragon till all your plans are ended.

I am the garuda,
Born full grown.
No perch, no nest, no place to rest;
The sky alone is my home.

With that the great bird lowered its mighty back and waited for her to climb on. Iliana stood still. She wasn't so sure about this. "Where are we going?" she asked.

Cawing loudly, the garuda sang:

> *To the clouds—*
> *To the sky—*
> *Beyond all you see.*
> *I'll take you to where*
> *You most want to be.*

Iliana gave a last look at the horizon to see if maybe the dragon had come back, but saw only the rising sun. Gathering all her courage, she stepped on one half of the broken rock and climbed the garuda's mighty back. She felt the great bird lift beneath her and glide over the cliff as they swooped down into the mists below. And then, as the garuda caught the wind in its wings, they soared upward! Flying! Soaring into the blue sky! The garuda's flight was her flight. Its wings were her wings. Iliana wondered if the dragon was still there—invisible in all that blueness. Maybe they were flying right through him. Or maybe he had gone to some far-off place. It did not seem to matter now. Iliana no longer cared if she found the sun. The notion of getting somewhere seemed meaningless to her. The pennant on her helmet played in the wind; her boots pressed into the garuda's feathers. And finally, after hours or days or years of flying in this way, a land of rock mountains arose from nowhere in the midst of empty sky. Without landing, the garuda let Iliana slide gently off of its back to the rocky ground below. Circling in the sky, the garuda cried:

> *Hail to Iliana, the brave young warrior!*
> *Welcome to the Land of the Sun.*
> *Here you will meet the Dragon,*
> *Here your quest will be won.*

Iliana watched as the garuda circled higher and higher until it faded from view. When she looked down, she found that she was now fully dressed in armor with a gold breastplate, an apron of gold chain mail and a bright yellow sun medallion blazing from the center of her chest. The armor was strong. Nothing could harm it. And yet, it made her feel exposed and vulnerable, as if her body were somehow turned inside out and she wore her heart on the outside. Being dressed in this armor brought to her lips the warrior's cry. As she stood with her arms stretched out to the sky, she shouted again and again:

"KI KI SO SO!"

liana looked around her. Something about this place seemed familiar. The rocks and junipers reminded her of the mountains that surrounded the Kalapa Valley where she lived. How strange that the Land of the Sun should look so much like her homeland! Wandering through the rocky ravines and hillsides of the Land of the Sun, she soon came to the edge of a wide valley, a valley filled with houses and buildings. In the middle, on a large hill, was a palace. Iliana could not believe her eyes. She was looking down upon the Kalapa Valley. "The garuda didn't bring me to the Land of the Sun. It brought me home! I must see the king and queen at once!"

Iliana climbed down the hillside and started to walk toward the palace. Everything looked the same as when she left. The people still looked worried; they still walked with their heads down and nobody smiled except for Iliana. She felt strong in her boots, she felt cheerful in her helmet, and she felt ready for anything in her suit of armor. As she passed by people stopped what they were doing to watch her. One by one they began to follow her and soon there was a whole crowd of people walking along behind her.

At the gates of the palace, the guards were amazed to see a young girl dressed in such fine armor. "I've come to see the king and queen," Iliana announced. From the courtyard one of the guards led her into the palace and up a long flight of stairs. Leaving her in an anteroom he disappeared through heavy wooden doors elaborately carved with tigers, lions, garudas, and dragons. After a short time, the guard returned to lead her through the same doors into a large sitting room.

Iliana bowed deeply as she entered. When she rose from her bow, she saw the king and queen sitting on beautifully carved ebony thrones. The king—dressed in a yellow robe—held a fan folded on his lap. His black hair was combed straight back from his face, which radiated friendliness. Overwhelmed by his presence, Iliana said to herself, "He is like the tiger, lion, garuda, and dragon all together in one person."

The queen—dignified and beautiful—was dressed in a purple robe. Her long black hair was pulled into a knot on the top of her head. Her gentle smile told Iliana that here sat the kindest person in all the world.

The king and queen greeted her warmly. It seemed to Iliana that they had been expecting her. She knelt on the floor before them and told them about her journey—about the tiger's walk, the lion's mane, and the flight of the garuda. She ended her story saying, "Your Majesties, I am sorry that I did not complete my quest. I wish that I had found a way to make the days grow longer."

The king smiled gently. "Young warrior, you have not failed. You have found the sun—not the sun in the sky, but the sun inside you. The warriors of old called this the Great Eastern Sun. It is the sun of human dignity, the sun of the warrior's tender heart. I sent my warriors and scholars to find what you have found, but they lacked your courage and imagination. Although you are young, you have shown genuine fearlessness. Although you have no formal training, you have exhibited the true qualities of a warrior. Iliana, you have brought the sun of basic wisdom home to our kingdom."

Summoning his guard, the king requested that all of the subjects of the kingdom be invited to gather outside the palace. From his balcony, he recounted Iliana's adventure to the large crowd. He enjoined them: "Subjects of Shambhala, this is a wonderful day. We have rediscovered the goodness of the sun in our hearts. Let us celebrate this goodness now, on this very day. Even if the days are short, we can have enormous cheerfulness within. Even if the nights are long, there is no shortage of light. Let candles burn in every window, for this shall be a festival of light in the time of darkness. Decorate your homes with bows of evergreen, a symbol of life in the dead of winter."

The queen added, "Since this celebration has been inspired by a child, we shall call this day Children's Day and all the children of the kingdom shall receive gifts from the king and queen."

It was a glorious celebration that went far into the night. Bonfires blazed on the hillsides and the scent of evergreen and juniper filled the air. There was laughter and singing and dancing and storytelling and all of the children received gifts, just as the queen had said.

The king, who was famous for his spontaneous songs, stood before the gathering and sang:

Your heart is tender, sad and true.
No brighter sun can be shown to you.
The light of day will come and go,
But the light of tender heart will grow.

It will grow as slowly as an ancient tree.
It will fly like a bird that is suddenly free.
Like the rising sun that ends the night,
A tender heart is forever bright.

Iliana was the center of attention. Everyone wanted to talk to her. She told her story again and again by the fire until finally, in the early hours of the morning, she fell asleep in her mother's arms. As the eastern sky was beginning to blush with dawn, Iliana's father carried her home. When they reached their house she woke up and asked her father to put her down. She wanted to see the sunrise.

Iliana climbed a small hill behind the house. By the time she reached the top, the sun was an orange globe perched on a bank of rose-colored clouds on the horizon. Iliana lay on her back in a patch of dried winter grass and gazed into the blue sky above. The day promised to be bright and clear and crisp.

Now slowly from the open sky appeared the faint outline of a dragon's head. At first Iliana thought that she was imagining it, but as the lines became more clear, she began to see the dragon's mouth and eyes and the long coils of its body until a clear image of a dragon filled the sky. And now suddenly this image came to life. The dragon was breathing and moving about. Its enormous head loomed directly above her and its jade green eyes moved quickly—looking in all directions. Its gaping red mouth seemed to smile, somehow all the while looking fierce and powerful. The rolling sound of thunder filled the sky.

The dragon stayed there clearly in the sky for a few minutes and then, as suddenly as it had come to life, it once again became still and started to fade—first the body, then the head. Then once again, Iliana was looking up at a featureless blue sky. But when she stood up she found that she was holding a crystal sword in her right hand. She offered it to the sky, in a salute to the invisible dragon. As the dragon's sword gleamed in the sunlight, it seemed to be alive, vibrating with power. Yet she knew that this sword could never be used for fighting or getting her own way. It was the sword of confidence and kindness. As she placed it in its sheath and started down the hill, she felt that her journey was just beginning.

Once in her room, Iliana placed her boots side by side on the floor and then carefully arranged her helmet, armor, and sword on a high shelf where she kept her special things. As she got ready for bed, she decided never to tell anyone about seeing the dragon. "It's best not to go too far with stories," she told herself as she settled into bed and drifted off into a long, dreamless sleep.

EPILOGUE

he next day was a tiny bit longer and the day after that was longer still. For months after the celebration, the days continued to grow longer until Midsummer's Day, the longest day of all. After that, the days began to grow shorter again until the next December.

Many people have speculated about why the sun changed its course in the sky that year. The king's scientists said it had something to do with the earth shifting on its axis. Others said that the dragon had decided to make the days grow short in the winter so that people can remember their hearts and stop to celebrate inner wisdom on the cold, dark days of December. Still others said that that is just the way things are, and that is that.

But whatever the reason, it has stayed that way to this very day. And so in late December, when the sun sets early and the winds blow cold, we know it's time to decorate our homes with evergreen and candles, and to celebrate the magic of childhood and the goodness of the Great Eastern Sun.

The Tiger's Song

I am the ti-ger, I walk on the ground. I roam thru the jun-gle, I move with-out a sound.

I am the ti-ger, I glide thru the trees. I move thru the jun-gle as soft as a breeze. I

roam on the earth and all thru the night with smiles all a-long my back I fill the sky with light.

I am the ti-ger, I walk on the ground. I am the ti-ger with smiles all a-round. If you

try too hard to hurry you will al-ways lag be-hind, but if you want to walk like me you must al-ways take your time. Con-

tin-ue on your quest, young girl, tho your challenges — are great. But don't for-get the jun-gle path or the

ti-ger's gen-tle gait. What you've learned so far will guide you as you journey far from home. So

take this gift re-mem-ber me as you ven-ture on a-lone.

THE LION'S SONG

I am the li—on white as snow this cheer-ful world— is all I know.

Wel-come to— my mountain lair where I roam the high—lands free from care.

All day long I've watched you walking steady— as a ti-ger stalk-ing.

But your face is sad, your brow is stern, There's something else that you must learn.

Your pace is good—, your legs are strong, but something in— your back is wrong. Your

shoul-ders droop, your head is low, you don't en-joy— the mountain snow.

The snow is— fresh, the sky is clear, there's nothing— in the world to fear

So listen— well to what I've said, Re—lax your shoul-ders, lift your head:

2x:

I am the per—ky li—on, I play the whole day long, In

all my life I ne-ver give up I sing the cheer— ful song.

THE GARUDA SONG

SKY, EARTH AND ME

Where-ev-er I walk, the sky moves with me, Great clouds like ships sail-ing at sea, where-

ev-er I step the ground moves with me, We trav-el to-geth-er, sky earth and me. How

tall is my hel-met how high is the sky—, How far will I walk on this path by 'n

by—. How tall is my hel-met how high is the sky—, How far will I walk on this path by 'n

by—.

TENDER HEART

Your heart is ten-der sad and true, No brigh-ter sun can be shown to you. The

light of day will come and go, The light of ten-der heart will grow. It will

grow as slow-ly as an an-cient tree, It will fly like a bird that is sudden-ly free. Like the

ris—ing sun that ends the night, A ten-der heart is for-ev-er bright.

36

WALTER FORDHAM found his inspiration for Iliana in the Children's Day holiday, held each year in December by the Shambhala community of meditation practitioners, of which he is a member. This holiday, instituted by Chögyam Trungpa Rinpoche, celebrates children and childhood, emphasizing that every child can be a king or a queen. As a father to two girls and twin boys, Walter decided to fulfill a request that had been made long ago for him to tell "the story" of Children's Day. In addition to being a talented singer and storyteller, Walter is a poet whose work has appeared in *New Directions, International Anthology of Prose and Poetry*. Iliana is his first book.

Walter was born and raised in New Jersey and studied English Literature at Guilford College. He now makes his home with his wife Joanne and children Catherine, Alicia, Peter, and William in Halifax, Nova Scotia.

TATJANA KRIZMANIC creates brilliant pastel drawings and oil paintings whose swirling playful intensity draws out the joyfulness of everyday life. Tatjana claims the world of music as her inspiration, seeing her works as "silent sounds that sing and dance across the canvas." During the 1980s she created artistic works for friends and patrons, while also working as a commercial art director. Since her first exhibit in Boulder, Colorado, she has built a strong following. Her paintings reside in numerous private collections and are shown in galleries and museums in the United States, Canada, and Europe. She teaches at the Nova Scotia College of Art and Design and has recently completed a number of children's books for American and Canadian publishers.

A native of the former Yugoslavian republic of Croatia, Tatjana studied linguistics and languages at the University of Zagreb and at Georgetown University. She now lives in Halifax, Nova Scotia, with her husband Peter and daughters Emelia and Katja.